Where **Oil** Come From?

C. Vance Cast

Illustrated by Sue Wilkinson

BARRON'S

Hi. I'm Clever Calvin. My Aunt Linda is taking my cat Mel and me to an oil refinery close to her home in Tulsa, Oklahoma. She thinks this is a good chance for us to learn about the importance of oil and where it comes from.

The car we are driving in needs gasoline to run.
Gasoline is a fuel made from oil. Home heating fuel is
made from oil, too.

Many other products are also made from oil. Can you think of any? Oil is used to make...
asphalt for paving the roads we drive on...

diesel fuel for trucks, buses,

and trains...

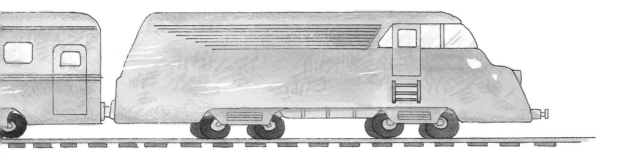

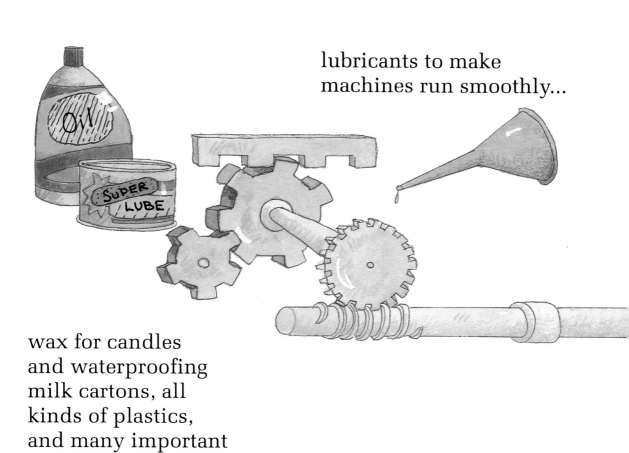

lubricants to make machines run smoothly...

wax for candles and waterproofing milk cartons, all kinds of plastics, and many important chemical products.

The scientific name for this kind of oil is *petroleum*. Petroleum is very important because it supplies the world with products used in industry, transportation, and in our homes. But where does it come from?

Let's go inside the refinery museum where we can see exhibits that explain what oil is and how it is found.

Most scientists agree that the story of petroleum started over 100 million years ago, when the Earth was almost all covered by seas and oceans. This was even before the dinosaurs.

Petroleum was formed from tiny marine plants and animals called *plankton*, along with larger plants and animals that had died and drifted to the bottom of the sea.

Their remains were covered by layers of mud and sand that washed into the seas from the shore. Many such layers, called *sediments*, were piled up this way. The process could have taken millions of years.

Because of the movements of the Earth's crust, the mud and sand layers were folded and squeezed, causing extreme heat and pressure.

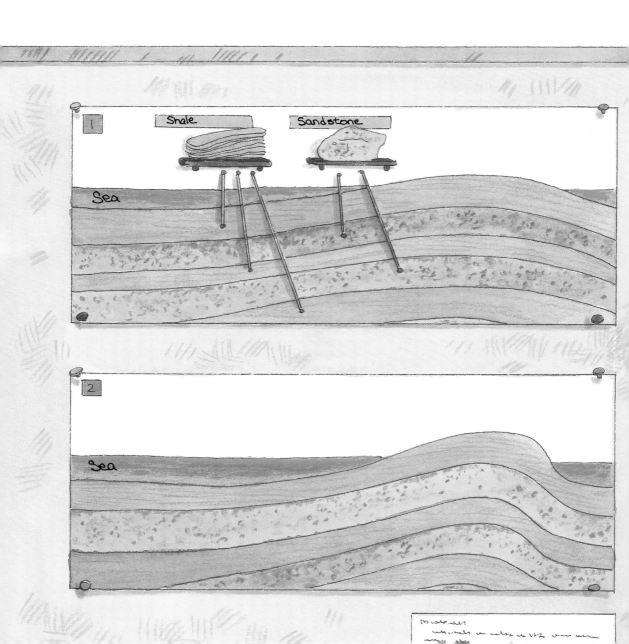

This heat and pressure gradually turned the layers of sediment into different kinds of rocks. Some of those rocks were solid, but some had tiny holes, or pores. Rocks with holes, which include sandstone and limestone, are called *porous rocks*.

Slowly, the layers of plant and animal remains were chemically changed. Because of bacteria, heat, and pressure of the overlying rock, they were transformed into oil and gas. This oil and gas seeped and flowed through the holes in the porous rocks until they reached a layer of shale, which is a nonporous rock.

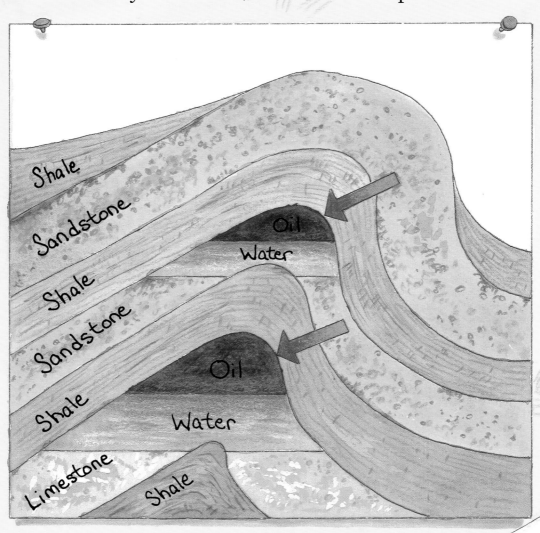

Here, the gas and oil were trapped. These pools (or *traps*) of oil and gas are where petroleum is found today. But it is not an easy job locating these traps, because they are far beneath the ground and can't be seen.

So how do we find them?

Looking for petroleum is called exploring or *prospecting*. The people who explore are called prospectors. Prospectors don't do their work alone, though. They get help from scientists who study the Earth, including *geologists* and *geophysicists*.

Geologists help by making maps of the Earth that show where porous rock such as sandstone and limestone are. With these maps prospectors can tell where petroleum traps are most likely to be found.

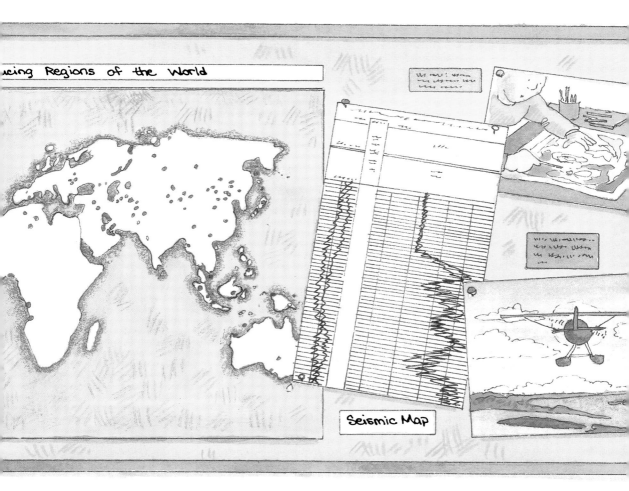

Geologists even fly in airplanes—that run on fuel made from oil, of course—to check on how the Earth's surface looks.

Then, geophysicists often use a technique called *reflection seismology*. Using reflection seismology they can tell something about the nature of the rock layers deep within the Earth. Here's how.

First, the scientists make loud sound waves below the Earth's surface. Usually dynamite is exploded under the ground, but sometimes big *thumper trucks* are used to make the sound waves. These trucks have giant pads that vibrate and strike the ground over and over again.

The sound waves travel down through the Earth and are reflected back up to the surface of the Earth by layers of rock deep under the ground. By placing microphones called *geophones* in different places on the ground, an instrument called a *seismograph* can record and measure the reflected sound waves.

Since the sound waves are different when reflected off rock that contains gas and oil, geophysicists are usually able to tell the prospector if there is oil in the area.

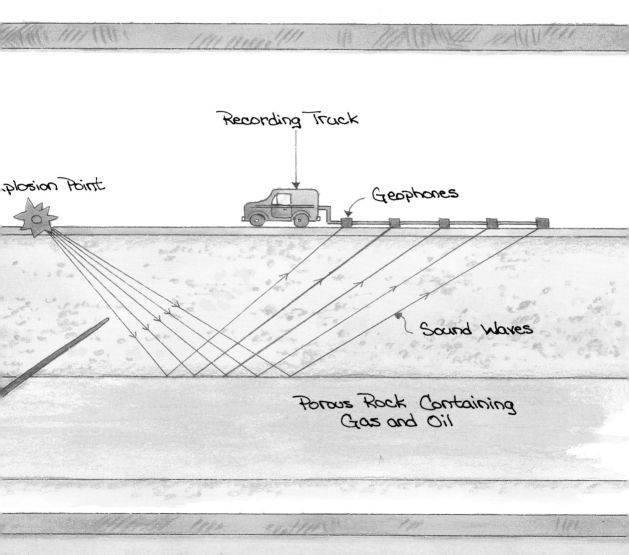

Recording Truck

Explosion Point

Geophones

Sound Waves

Porous Rock Containing Gas and Oil

Even though prospectors have help from all these scientists, the only way to be sure there is oil is to drill a hole through the rock. When prospectors drill in a new area, they are *wildcatting*. Sometimes they strike oil...

and sometimes the well is dry. Out of every ten wells drilled, only one yields enough oil to collect.

First a steel tower, called a *derrick*, is erected.

The drilling rig lowers a drill bit on the end of a turning drill pipe. The bit cuts a hole in the ground and through the rock.

These drills are a lot like the ones used to drill wells for water. The drill bit may have thousands of tiny sharp diamonds for its cutting edge.

As the well is drilled, the drilling team lines it with steel pipe called *casing*. The casing keeps the sides of the well from falling in, and it keeps any underground water out.

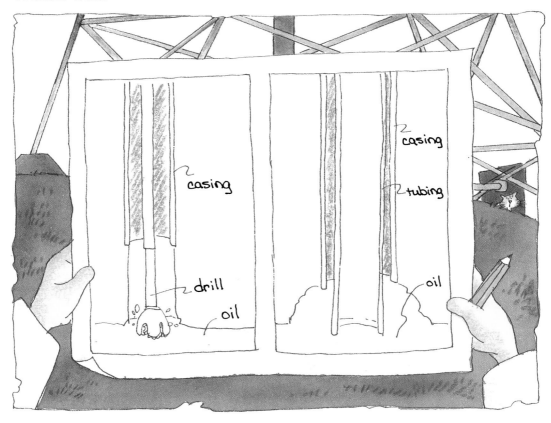

When the well is deep enough, tubing is placed inside the casing so the oil will have a way to get to the surface. Most wells are about 6,000 feet (1,800 meters) deep, but they could be over 20,000 (6,100 meters) feet deep! Oil wells can cost millions of dollars to drill.

When the tubing is in place, meters and valves are placed on the top to control and measure the flow of the oil.

Usually the natural pressure is strong enough to make the oil flow to the surface. But sometimes the pressure in the well is not enough, so pumps must be used to force the oil to the surface.

Once the oil gets to the top of the well, it passes through a *separator*. The separator removes the gases and water. Then the *crude oil* can be pumped into gathering tanks, where it is stored until it is transported to a refinery.

Crude oil can be carried from the oil fields to refineries by tanker trucks, railroad cars, or pipelines. You've probably seen tanker trucks like this one on the highway.

Sometimes pipelines carry the crude oil through mountains, under fields, deserts, swamps, and ice.

One long pipeline is called the Little Big Inch. The Little Big Inch carries oil all the way from the Texas oil fields to New Jersey, a distance of more than 1,500 miles (2,400 kilometers)!

Maintaining all this pipeline takes hard work.
Inspectors in helicopters and inspectors walking on
foot must examine it constantly.

The inspectors check to see if the pipe has been damaged by ice, snow, or rain, or if people are digging or building too close to the line. They also inspect all the machines and instruments along the pipeline that record leaks, oil flow, and other conditions.

Once the crude oil reaches the refinery it is heated until much of it turns to vapor. The hot oil vapor then passes into a *fractionating tower* where it is separated into different parts to make different products.

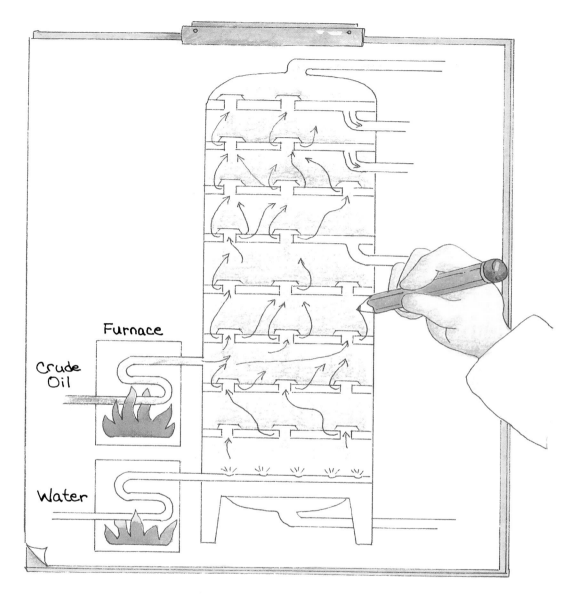

Furnace

Crude
Oil

Water

The tower has a series of trays with holes in them.
When the hot oil vapor passes through these trays on
its way to the top of the tower, the vapor condenses
(turns back into liquid) and settles on them.

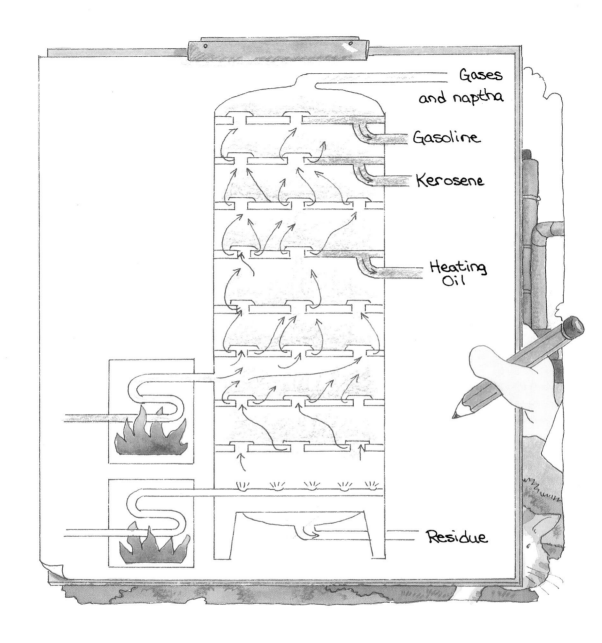

Gases and naptha

Gasoline

Kerosene

Heating Oil

Residue

Each tray of condensed oil vapor is used for different products, such as kerosene and heating oils. The highest tray in the tower is used to make gasoline.

The different petroleum products are then taken from the refinery to the companies that use or sell them to us. And the gasoline is transported to gas stations all over the country.

Aunt Linda, Mel, and I are going to drive home now. When we get there, I'll show you some experiments with oil that you can do yourself.

Oil and water don't mix — and in this experiment you can prove it!

First, get a glass jar with a tight lid. Fill it half full with water.

Then add a couple drops of food coloring.

Finally, pour in an eighth of a cup of cooking oil.

Does the oil float on top of the colored water? Why?

Now put the lid on the jar.
Make sure it is tight.

Turn the jar upside down.
Does the oil still go to the
top of the water?

What happens if you try
to shake up the mixture?
Does it reseparate?

Add a half cup of laundry detergent, cover tightly, and shake the mixture again.

What happens now? If you let the mixture stand for a while, do the layers reseparate?

Wow! Science experiments are fun. I hope you enjoyed doing this one. Bye for now.

Glossary

casing Tubes that are used for lining the inside of the well.

crude oil Oil as it is pumped from the ground before it is transported to a refinery.

derrick A big frame built over a well to hold the drill bit.

fractionating tower A tower used to separate crude oil into different parts, including gasoline, kerosene, and heating oil.

geologists, geophysicists Scientists who study the formation of the Earth.

geophones Microphones used to hear vibrations in the ground.

petroleum A flammable liquid that is formed far under the Earth's surface.

plankton Tiny animal and plant organisms that drift in the ocean.

porous rock Rock that has tiny holes through which gas and liquid can pass.

prospecting Searching for gas and oil deposits.

reflection seismology A way of measuring how sound waves are reflected through the Earth to determine what kind of rock is underneath.

sediment Sand and other material that settles to the bottom of liquid.

seismograph An instrument used to measure vibrations in the ground.

separator A device that removes water and vapor from crude oil.

thumper truck A truck with a giant pad that is used to strike the ground to make sound waves.

traps (petroleum traps) A place beneath the surface of the Earth where oil and gas are caught by a layer of nonporous rock.

wildcatting Drilling for oil in an area that has not been previously explored.

International Standard Book No. 0-8120-1467-7

Library of Congress Catalog Card No. 93-10732

PRINTED IN HONG KONG

3456   9927   987654321

Library of Congress Cataloging-in-Publication Data
Cast, C. Vance.
    Where does oil come from? / by C. Vance Cast ; illustrated by Sue Wilkinson.
        p.   cm.
    Summary: Explains in simple terms where and how oil is found, extracted, refined, and made into many other products.
    ISBN 0-8120-1467-7
    1. Petroleum—Juvenile literature. 2. Petroleum products—Juvenile literature. [1. Petroleum. 2. Petroleum industry and trade.]
    I. Wilkinson, Sue (Susan), ill. II. Title.
TN870.3.C37 1993   93-10732
553.2'82—dc20   CIP
                                                     AC